Weekly Reader Children's Book Club presents

Hound and Bear

story and pictures by Dick Gackenbach

A Clarion Book

THE SEABURY PRESS · NEW YORK

for Dorothy

The Seabury Press, 815 Second Avenue, New York, N.Y. 10017

LIBRARY OF CONGRESS CATALOGING IN PUBLICATION DATA

Gackenbach, Dick.   Hound and Bear.
"A Clarion book."
SUMMARY: Hound and Bear are very good friends until Hound
plays one practical joke too many.
[1. Friendship—Fiction. 2. Dogs—Fiction.
3. Bears—Fiction] I. Title.
PZ7.G117Ho   [E]   76-3525   ISBN 0-8164-3170-1

Weekly Reader Children's Book Club Edition

The Long Night

Bear and Hound
were best friends.
Bear was very sensible.
Hound was very silly.
"What a good joke it
would be on Bear,"
Hound thought,
"if I painted his
bedroom window
black."

That night, after Bear
went to sleep,
Hound put black paint
on all the panes
in Bear's window.
Next morning the
sun was shining bright.
But when Bear woke up
and looked out
of his window,
everything
was very
black.

"It is still nighttime," Bear yawned.

He went back to bed and fell asleep.

When he woke up again, it was

12 o'clock noon.

He peeked out of his window

for some sign of morning.

"How black the night is,"

he said.

Bear lit his candle
and looked at his old
pocket watch.
Both hands were
at twelve.
"Why, it's only midnight,"
Bear said. He blew out
the candle, and went
back to bed again.
Bear slept through the
day and all through
the night.

 When Bear woke up
the next morning,
he was very hungry.
"I could eat a bear!"
he said.

"But it is not yet time for breakfast."
His room was very dark.
So Bear sat up in bed, thinking about
a good breakfast
of bread and honey.
"Hm-m-m," he thought,
as he waited for the sun to rise.

Hound came to Bear's house and pounded
on the door.

"Wake up, Bear," he shouted, "wake up!"

"I am awake," said Bear from his bed.

"I am waiting for the sun to shine."

"The sun is shining, you ninny Bear."

Hound laughed and laughed.

Bear went to see why Hound was laughing.

When he opened the door his eyes

blinked in the bright sun.

He looked at the ladder and the black paint,

and at his black window.

"It's one of your tricks, Hound," he said.

Bear went back into his house. Hound

came too, laughing until his sides hurt.

Bear sat down and began to eat a big cake.

"How long was I asleep?" he asked.

"All through yesterday," giggled Hound.

"Then," said Bear,

"I have missed your birthday, Hound!"

Hound stopped laughing.

He had forgotten his own birthday.

"I was going to have a surprise

party for you," said Bear.

"Oh my," said Hound,

sadly.

"And that was your cake
I just ate," said Bear,
swallowing the last piece.
"Oh dear," said Hound.
Hound loved birthday
cakes and parties.
"That was a great cake,"
said Bear.
"Now I think I'll take
a nap."

The Package

One fall day, Hound asked Bear,
"What are you going
to do today?"
"I am going to wait for
the Postman to bring a very
important package," Bear replied.

"And what are you going to do, Hound?"
Bear asked.

"Clean my house and wash my socks,"
answered Hound.

"Those are good things to do," said Bear.

"Yes," said Hound, "but I would rather
play a game of pretend."

"Oh," said Bear, "pretend what?"

"I would go to your house and

pretend that I am you,"

said Hound.

"And what would I do?" asked Bear.

"You could go to my house and

pretend that you are me,"

Hound explained.

So Bear went to Hound's house

and pretended he was Hound.

Bear cleaned the dirty house,

and washed all the dirty socks.

Hound went to Bear's house
and pretended he was Bear.
He ate all of Bear's
cookies and jelly beans.
Then he drank all
of Bear's root beer.
When the Postman
came with the package,
Hound thought it would
be a good joke on Bear
if he sent the
package back.

"Bear told me to send the package back,"

Hound told the Postman.

The Postman took a big crayon and marked

on the package, "RETURN TO SENDER."

So Bear's package was on its

way back to the store.

Soon Bear came home.

"Did you do everything I was going to do?"

asked Hound.

"Yes," said Bear, "I cleaned your house."

"Did you wash socks?" asked Hound.

"Yes," said Bear. "And what did you do, Hound?"

he asked.

"I ate your cookies,"
said Hound.

"Well," said Bear, "that's
what I would have done."

"I drank all your root beer,"
said Hound.

"I would have done that too,"
said Bear.

"And I sent your package back."
Hound burst out laughing.

"I would not have done that,"
Bear said.

"It was a sweater I bought

for you," said Bear.

"Oh," said Hound.

"Yes," said Bear,

"you will wish you had

it when it gets cold."

"Oh dear, oh dear,"

said Hound, sadly.

"Furthermore," said Bear,

"that's the last game

I will play with you!"

The Best Present

Hound knocked on

Bear's door.

"Open up, Bear," he shouted.

"I have something for you."

"Is it one of your tricks again?"

Bear asked from behind the door.

"No trick, I promise,"

said Hound.

When Bear opened the door

Hound gave him a big

box all tied in

ribbon.

"Open it, it's for you," said Hound.

Bear opened it very slowly for he was sure something

would pop out and hit him in the nose.

Inside the package was a smaller one

all tied in ribbon, too.

"You have tricked me too many times," said Bear.

"Trust me," said Hound.

So Bear opened this

package with even greater

care.

He was sure it would explode.

But inside was an even smaller

box all tied

in ribbon.

"If this is another trick,

you will lose my friendship forever,"

said Bear.

"Your friendship is very dear to me,"

said Hound.

So Bear opened
the last package.
Inside was
a beautiful hat,
with a real
goose feather
in the band.
"Thank you,"
said Bear.
He was
very pleased.

"I was sure it was another trick," Bear said.

"I promise never to play another trick
on you," said Hound.

"That," sighed Bear, "is the best present
of all."

Then they both went to town so everyone
could see Bear's new hat.